15.50 n. d.

LET'S VISIT
A Chocolate Factory

by Catherine O'Neill

photography by James W. Parker

Troll Associates

Library of Congress Cataloging in Publication Data

O'Neill, Catherine, (date)
    Let's visit a chocolate factory.

    Summary: Takes the reader to a factory where cocoa
beans are processed into chocolate products such as
cocoa powder, chocolate chips, and bars for baking.
    1. Chocolate processing—Juvenile literature.
2. Chocolate—Juvenile literature. [1. Chocolate
processing. 2. Chocolate] I. Parker, James W., ill.
II. Title.
TP640.O54   1988   664'.5   87-3460
ISBN 0-8167-1161-5 (lib. bdg.)
ISBN 0-8167-1162-3 (pbk.)

The author and publisher wish to thank Richard McCarty and General Foods Manufacturing Corporation,
James Robinson of Robinson's Fine Candies, Rocky Hill, NJ, and Our Sundae Best, Bordentown, NJ,
for their outstanding assistance and cooperation.

It's Saturday morning—the perfect time to make a batch of chocolate chip cookies! But have you ever wondered how the *chocolate chips* are made? Let's visit a chocolate factory to find out.

Chocolate products are made from the beans of the *cacao tree*. The trees grow in hot, rainy parts of the world such as Central and South America. There the beans are packed in burlap sacks and exported to other countries. Today we say "cocoa," because long ago someone misspelled "cacao."

Workers at the factory unload the sacks. Then they slit each one open. The bags are full of raw cocoa beans. In their raw form they don't taste very good! The beans must be roasted, ground up, and mixed with sweeteners to taste like *chocolate*. After the beans are unloaded, a *conveyor belt* carries them into the factory.

A worker adjusts dials on the *roasting machine* that roasts the cocoa beans. The roasting beans make a popping sound as their paper-thin husks come loose. Next, a *cracker-fanner machine* separates the husks from the beans. A large fan blows the husks away. Then the beans are cracked into nibs. The nibs, or small pieces of cocoa bean, are used to make the chocolate.

The nibs fill many huge storage tanks at the factory. The tanks keep them fresh until they are ground in the factory's *grinding machines.* As the nibs are ground, they turn into a liquid called *chocolate liquor.* The liquor has a strong chocolate flavor, but one that is bitter, not sweet.

The chocolate liquor is then separated into the two main ingredients of chocolate: *cocoa butter* and *cocoa powder.* High pressure inside the cocoa press forces cocoa butter to run out. The clear liquid is then collected and allowed to harden.

Large pressed cakes of cocoa powder remain, once the liquid is removed. The cakes pop out of the cocoa press and are carried off on a conveyor belt. Later, the cakes will be cooled, ground up, and sifted into cocoa powder.

An inspector checks the sifted powder to make sure it has been finely ground. If the cocoa powder passes inspection, it is funneled into paper bags. A worker weighs each bag on a scale—each one should hold fifty pounds. The cocoa powder will be sold to a company that makes hot chocolate mix.

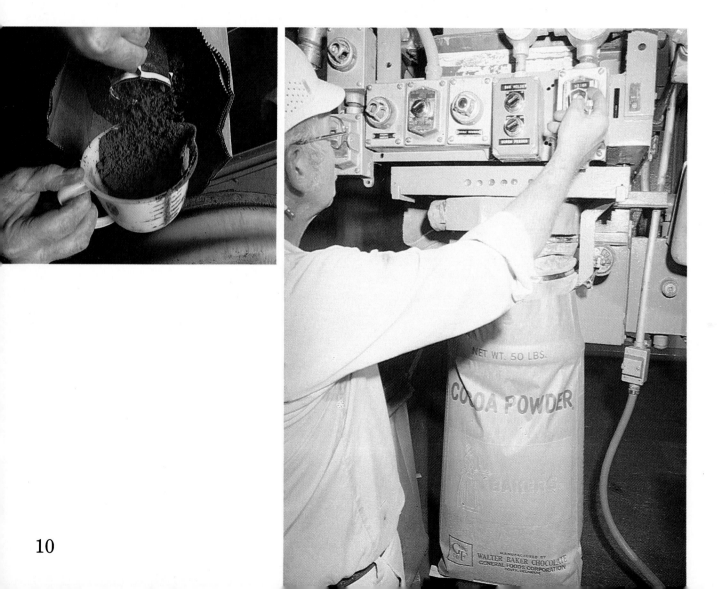

Another worker seals each bag with a heavy-duty sewing machine. The bags are then piled onto platforms where fork lifts will carry them off to be stored.

In another part of the factory, chocolate is
made in a *conching machine*. Chocolate liquor,
cocoa butter, sugar, and milk are combined in
these large mixing bowls. The metal drum is
heated to about 130° Fahrenheit—just the right
temperature to melt the mixture as a worker
watches from above.

Now it's time to mold different mixtures into different shapes. Some, such as small chocolate chips or bars, can be found in grocery stores. Others, such as ten-pound chocolate blocks, are sold to candy and ice-cream makers.

Some ice-cream parlors make their own ice cream and their own candy, too. How many ice-cream flavors can you name that use chocolate as an ingredient?

Whether it's mint chip or rocky road, it tastes better with hot fudge on top! The delicious chocolate sauce was made by the owner of this ice-cream parlor.

At the back of the store, a special *white chocolate* recipe is being prepared. Just like dark chocolate, the recipe combines cocoa butter, sweeteners, and other ingredients. But unlike dark chocolate, this special mixture does not include cocoa powder. The mixing bowl sits in a tub of hot water to keep the chocolate warm and melted.

The melted mixture of white chocolate will be used to make Easter bunnies. With a large ladle, the mixture is poured into one half of the mold. The candy maker then pours the other half and clamps the two halves together.

He shakes the filled mold so the chocolate blends together. Then it is refrigerated. After the chocolate has cooled and hardened, the clamps are removed from the mold. Out pops the bunny from its plastic mold—just in time for Easter!

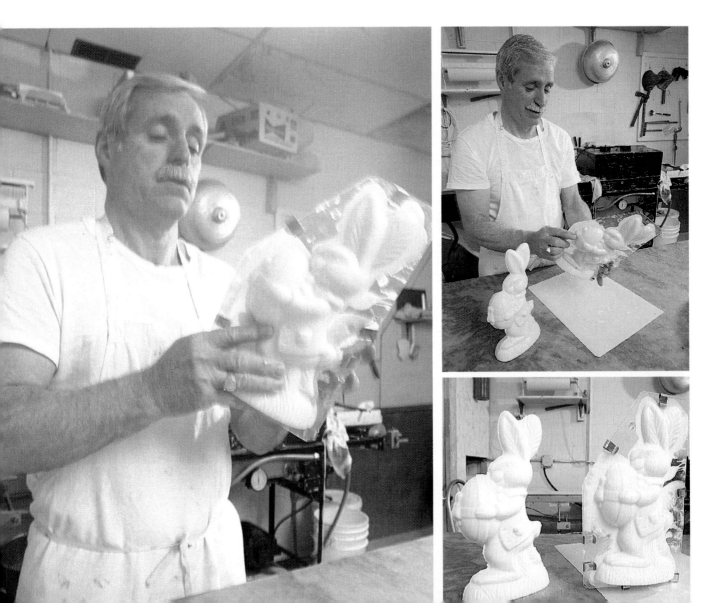

All sorts of chocolate and candy treats are sold in this neighborhood store. Have you ever tasted fresh berries and fruit dipped in homemade chocolate? The candy makers buy the chocolate ingredients from the chocolate factory.

Back at the factory, a machine called a
depositor squirts warm, melted chocolate into
molds. Each squirt deposits just the right amount
to fill a mold for a small bar of chocolate. The
molds move through a refrigerated tunnel where
they harden into bars. The bars then move along
a conveyor belt on their way to be wrapped.

Bright green wrappers are joined together on a roll at the end of the machine. The roll is fed into a cutting machine that separates the wrappers. The machine then covers each bar with its wrapper—no one has touched the chocolate! The process of mixing, molding, and wrapping has all been done by machine.

Wrapped bars come off the production line in the last stage of the chocolate-making process. Now it's time to pack the bars into cardboard boxes. The boxes will be shipped to grocery stores, which will then sell the chocolate to customers.

The company also makes small squares of chocolate used for baking at home. The workers check the baking chocolate to be sure that each square is perfect. Broken squares are tossed into a bin, melted down, and molded again.

A machine wraps each square of baking chocolate in tissue-thin white paper. Another worker checks the squares to be sure they've been properly wrapped. If they pass inspection, they are packaged in boxes in groups of eight.

To make chocolate chips, melted chocolate must stream through hundreds of tiny nozzles. The nozzles squeeze small drops of chocolate onto a metal conveyor belt. Each tiny drop of chocolate forms one warm, wet, shiny chocolate chip!

The chips begin to harden as they move away from the depositing machine. The machine can make one million chips per hour. How many chips can *you* eat?

The conveyor belt covered with chocolate chips also travels through a refrigerated tunnel. At the end of the tunnel, the chips fall over a roller and into a chute.

A bagging machine packages the chocolate chips that come out of the chute. When each bag is full, it is carefully sealed and dropped onto a slide. The slide meets another conveyor belt that carries the bags off to be boxed.

Finally, the bags of chocolate chips arrive on the grocery-store shelf. A mother and daughter select a bag to make chocolate chip cookies at home.

Here's a recipe for chocolate chip cookies that's easy and fun to make. Ask for permission to use the oven. Have a grownup help you set the oven temperature.

Chocolate Chip Cookies

Preheat oven to 375° F.

1. *Soften:*
   ½ cup butter or margarine

2. *Add gradually:*
   6 tablespoons brown sugar
   6 tablespoons white sugar

3. *Beat in:*
   1 egg
   ½ teaspoon vanilla

4. *Sift and stir in:*
   1 cup and
   2 tablespoons
   sifted flour
   ½ teaspoon salt
   ½ teaspoon baking soda

5. *Stir in:*
   ½ cup chocolate chips
   ½ cup chopped nuts (optional)

Drop the batter from a teaspoon onto a greased cookie sheet.

Bake for about 10 minutes.

The cookies are ready to come out of the oven. Now comes the best part of all—eating them up!